DANDYBOY

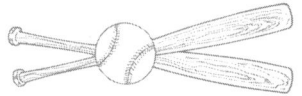

12/12/02

DANDYBOY

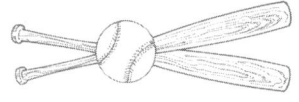

Franklin Hawkeye Melzer

Rutledge Books, Inc.  Danbury, CT

Rutledge Books, Inc.
107 Mill Plain Road, Danbury, CT 06811
1-800-278-8533
www.rutledgebooks.com

Manufactured in the United States of America

Library of Congress Cataloging in Publication Data
Melzer, Franklin
    Dandyboy

    ISBN: 1-58244-106-5

    1. Fiction.

Library of Congress Card Number: 00-109266

DEDICATION

These fables are dedicated to my nieces and nephews,
Stephanie, Rachel, Marci, Marissa, Michael
and especially to Danny whose wit and wisdom
and his profound sense of moment
inspired the telling of these stories.

PROLOGUE

"Joe D."

"Yeah, nobody covers the outfield the way he does—he just glides."

"Hey, how bout Ted Williams—forget about it who can hit like him?"

"Wait a second, you guys never saw anybody like Mickey Mantle—what power—what speed."

"I'll still take Joltin' Joe."

While growing up on Hope Street in the Town of Springdale, Danny listened to the stories; the debates, the arguments—his imagination fired up by the endless tales of glory, of triumph and tragedy. The exploits of Joe DiMaggio, The Mick and The Splendid Splinter were magnified by the storytellers, that gang of baseball aficionados who sat around Danny's house.

It was a time when baseball was the game that boys played and the game that men talked about. Was it the best of times or was it the worst of times? It was for Danny a time of imagination and dreams. The games that Danny played and dreamed about are not of any time; the lessons learned were for all time. Exact historical time is meaningless, insignificant. It was a time when young boys dreamed of glory, when parents and fans cheered as the boys took to the field to play the game of baseball.

During this era of imagination when sleep overtook Danny and dreams began, a young baseballer, Dandyboy, emerged. He played the game for the joy of the contest and yes, for the glory of winning. Mystically and mysteriously, Storymaster, a sage who was the embodiment of all who had argued and debated the game, would appear.

The Storymaster was Dandyboy's Guardfather, a man who seems to have played the game, read all the books, seen all the movies, illuminates the path Dandyboy is to travel with anecdotes and fable. In this world of dreams, in this era of imagination, Storymaster/Guardfather recalls the events of the past and retells them to Dandyboy so that the games and playing, winning and losing teach Dandyboy lessons that will prepare him for the journey of growing up.

It may have been the best of times.

DANDYBOY
AND THE PAYBACK
A Fable

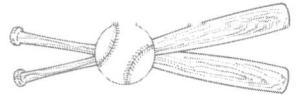

by: Franklin "Hawkeye" Melzer

—

In a time not long ago in the dale of spring on the street of Hope lived the baseballer named Dandyboy. His was a spirit of joy for Dandyboy played with the verve of yesteryear when those who played the game of ball loved the game above all else. Dandyboy was called a throw back.

He was a hurler of the curveball. Many batsmen had tried to strike the ball that curved but were unsuccessful. Dandyboy was fierce with the bat and his speed of foot on the bases paths made him a prince of thievery. Sometimes he wore the armor of the catcher when he was not hurling the ball that curved. He would catch the flame and fire of others who hurled and even sometimes the ball that curved. It was a position of importance for the base of home had to be protected, to prevent the scoring of runs. Dandyboy, with his arm of strength, had to gun down the thieves of bases as well. He loved to wear this suit of armor for only the bravest would take on this duty.

In this time of not long ago, the Galaxy I championship was to be played. Teams from the Galaxy sent their all-stars to compete. From far away came the boys from the field beyond the ridge, Wiltown sent its stars, as did the Walkers from Nor and the Darieners. Starford, however, was the heart of the galaxy and provided the most baseballers. Its teams were legendary and had produced prior champions. On this occasion there were six Starford teams. The Northrupters, the Stars of the North, the Natleos, the Rugamericans, the Jackisons, the Dalespringers, and the Federals.

The tournament featured the rule of the Phoenix for even if you faltered once you could rise from the ashes and win the grand prize. Few teams had ever had the fortitude to triumph after the initial loss.

"The Stars of the North are the favorites," said Dandyboy to the rest of his Dalespringer teammates at the end of practice.

"Well, Dandy, they are good, but the Natleos are better," responded Double A.

"No way, Double A, the Stars have Zack of the Home Run and Bigman, too," chimed in Dentistson.

"And Bigman throws from the left and with much fire," was Totalpauls's view.

"Well, I agree with Double A," shouted Gregnevermoan, the Natleos are awesome and Meglamike is the best ever!"

Coach Macramike quieted the boys, "Hey, forget about who is the best, we don't play them yet. We got to beat the Northrupters and Toga is pitching. Double A, get ready. Go warm up with Dandyboy."

Tournament play for the Dalespringers started with a contest against the Northrupters. The team traveled to the plains of Darien to stage the contest. Double A, the thrower of fire, was to pitch for the Dalespringers and Dandyboy was to don the suit of armor. It took great courage to accept the position behind the batter and receive the offering of the thrower of fire. The Northrupters were a scrappy team who also had a thrower of fire by the name of Toga. They did not appear to be awesome but many a galaxy team had fallen to them because the Northrupters never quit. If you became overconfident you could lose to the Northrupters.

Dentistson started things off well for the Dalespringers by lacing a double into left center field. The two runners on base scampered home to tally the first runs of the tournament. Double A was in control with the pitches of flames until the fourth inning when he could not place the ball within the zone of strikes. Many

Northrupters were put on base and the score became close.

Coach Macramike turned red with frustration.

"What's going on out there? Dandyboy, you've got to keep Double A focused," he shouted. "Dentistson, you and Gregnevermoan are dead out there, you've got to make some noise out there!!" yelled manager Jim Aged.

When the Dalespringers came to bat, their fans began to cheer. Two players reached base because the Northrupters pitcher became wild. The next batter was Gregnevermoan. He was a player of many positions and he never moaned when the coach told him to play at any location. He was also a hitter of long balls. With the count two balls and one strike, Gregnevermoan hit a three bagger and two runs scored.

In the remaining innings Double A was fearsome and the one batter who reached first base was thrown out by Dandyboy when the runner tried to steal second base. The Dalespringers had triumphed in the first game of the Galaxy I tournament.

Later that day while sitting in his room, Guardfather, the Storymaster, floated in.

"Dandyboy, You and the Dalespringers did well," greeted Guardfather.

"We did okay," responded Dandyboy "but the Stars of the North were awesome. Zack of the Home Run pounded the ball, they killed the Wiltowners."

"What about the Natleos?" asked Guardfather.

"Aw, it was no contest. Meglamike pitched and hit like a superstar. I don't think we can beat those teams," lamented Dandyboy.

"Come now my friend, that is not the right attitude, anything is possible if you believe," Guardfather offered. Dandyboy drifted off to sleep.

The following day the Dalespringers were to face Willie the Whiz, an undefeated, unstoppable player for the Benniewons.

He had been a dominating force in the Nor. Undaunted, the Dalespringers were ready for the challenge. Dandyboy once more was to play behind the plate of home. To pitch against the Benniewons was Dentistson.

In the first inning Dentistson was masterful, his fire was smoking and the ball that curved confused the Benniewons. They were set down one, two, three. In the Dalespringers' half of the inning the batters were of great strength and the ball, as if guided by radar, eluded the Benniewons who manned the positions of the field. Willy the Wiz was Willy the Whacked.

Dandyboy, with bases filled with Dalespringers, eyes concentrating on the pitch to be received, timed his magnificent swing perfectly and drove the ball over the center fielder's head. When the ball was retrieved and returned to the pitcher the bases were cleaned and Dandyboy was standing on third base. The smile on his face was an indication of the great joy that he had after fulfilling his obligation to drive the runners to the plate that is home. At the conclusion of the inning the Dalespringers had scored eight runs.

The day proved to be a disaster for the Benniewons. The game was completed after inning three when the Dalespringers led by the score of sixteen to zero.

There was much cheering by the fans. Friendlyfan, the most vocal of the Dalespringer loyalists shouted, "Our boys are the best, let's hear it for them."

A roar of approval followed, "Dalespringers! Dalespringers!" The team was running around and shouting as well.

Coach Macramike was concerned. He did not want the boys overconfident for that is the path to disaster.

"Dalespringers," he shouted, "into the dugout, on the double!"

When the shouting quieted down he said, "Okay, we won

two games and I'm proud of you, but the real tests are coming. Don't think you're the greatest yet! Our next game is against the Stars. Everyone has got to produce if we're going to beat them."

"What about the Natleos, how did they do?" asked Totalpaul.

"Stop worrying about them," manager Jim Aged angrily responded.

Coach Macramike, however, told the boys, "Okay boys, I know you're interested, but you've got to concentrate on one game at a time. Reyjose pitched the Natleos to victory over the Darieners and Meglamike got two hits."

The four remaining undefeated teams were the Federals, the Natleos, the Dalespringers, and the Stars of the North. Once more in the Galaxy Games Starford had proven to be dominant. Federal would play Natleo. The scheduled hurlers were Chrislingshot and Meglamike. It would be a game of much heat. In the Dalespringers/Stars of the North game, Double A would pitch against the Bigman, another game of pure speed and not much trickery.

Game day was ferociously hot. The leaves on the trees wilted. Neither the birds nor the bees took flight. People walked gingerly on the pavement parched by the blistering sun. The fans of each team sought shelter from the sun and disdained loyalty to the sidelines of their teams. All prayed that the players would not falter from the rays of the sun. The infield dust choked the players and the metal bats were hot.

Undaunted, the boys of summer took their positions on the field and game one commenced. It was a hard-fought contest. With Federal seemingly in control Natleo rallied to tie the score in the last inning.

"Extra innings," moaned the fans. They would now have to bake in the heat of the late afternoon. But what of the players? Miraculously none seemed to feel the effects of the day. After two extra innings Natleo scored to win the game.

In game two, Double A was peerless. His pitch of fire was untouchable. Somehow, however, a walk, a single, and an errant throw let a run blemish the effort of Double A. The Stars of the North led one to nothing. The batters of the Dalespringers, who had produced sixteen runs the game before, became impotent. The balls struck, which had eluded the fielders in days before, flew directly to the opposition. Bigman, too, seemed unstoppable.

Then Double A strode to the plate. He flexed his mighty arms. The heat had not withered this large young boy. One of Bigman's balls of fire was swatted back with great force and trajectory and sailed beyond the fence for a home run. If no one else would produce the hits for Double A, he would do so himself.

"Way to go," yelled Dandyboy as Double A rounded the bases.

Friendlyfan led the loyalists in cheering, "Dalespringers! Dalespringers!" The noise, however, was faint as the heat had taken the strength from the fans.

In the next inning the lads from the Dale performed miraculously in the field. Gregnevermoan was like an octopus ranging over the infield from his place at shortstop. He gunned out runners on what appeared to be impossible plays. Dandyboy, who had been moved to second base, roamed into right field to rob a Star of the North from a hit. He too covered the area assigned and threw out many a runner. Still, however, the bats were silent. Dandyboy walked two times as Bigman never gave him a pitch to hit. Each time, however, Dandyboy was left stranded.

In the meantime, the Stars of the North scored one run and led now two to one.

The usually quiet Totalpaul stood in front of the dugout. "Come on guys, we got to get a run, let's not lose," he pleaded.

Coach Macramike looked at the boys, he was sweating and

his clothes were wet. "I know it's hot Dalespringers, but you can do it. Everybody take a drink of water. Get your energy back."

The water worked like a miracle.

In the last inning two of the usually reliable hitters, Dentistson and Gregnevermoan, got on base. Double A came to bat. A hit would produce the two runs needed to win. So, on this day of sweltering heat, as the sun was fading in the west, unlike the hero of Mudville who failed to deliver, Double A hit a line drive into left center field and Dentistson and Gregnevermoan scored to win the game.

After the day of great excitement, Natleo would play the Dalespringers for the winner's bracket championship. Federal and the Stars of the North would have to battle back through the losers bracket to see if they could rise from the ashes as did the ancient phoenix.

The winner's game was scheduled for the next day. It would be a day of great pain and suffering and of great humiliation for the Dalespringers. A team, which had shown great courage in the previous galaxy games, collapsed.

Many speculated that the collapse came about because of the intimidation created by the aura of the Natleos and their boisterous fans.

The Natleos were a formidable appearing group. On their team was the giant Bucklehomer whose mere presence was intimidating. Although he did not hit the ball very often when he would strike it, it would sail out of the park or travel at such speed on the ground that it could knock over a boy. The real stars of the team were, however, Meglamike who could pitch and play shortstop better than anyone. He would usually produce the hit to beat you. Then there was Reyjose, the diminutive pitcher with all the junk and control. When he didn't pitch he would play center field. Finally there was Efrespo, their awesome first baseman and hitter of momentous drives.

In the first inning the Dalespringers batters were completely baffled by Reyjose. Two struck out and the third grounded out. Dentistson was pitching for the Dalespringers and the Natleo's wasted little time in hitting him. The first two batters hit wicked shots which fortunately for Dentistson were hit directly at the players. One was a hard ground ball to Dandyboy, who managed to knock it down and throw out the runner. The second was a line drive to the left fielder who caught it for an out.

But then disaster struck. Meglamike hit a double and Efrespo walked. Bucklehomer hit a hard bouncing ball at Dandyboy who seemed unsure of what to do. The ball eluded him. Two runs scored. Two more errors by the Dalespringers in the inning produced two more runs for the Natleos. Lawdmot, wearing the green and gold of the Natleos, rose and roared, "Kill the bums, they can't beat us! Send them back to the dale!"

Other fans cheered, "Yeah, send them home early, they're scared of you."

Friendlyfan shouted, "Don't give up Dalespringers," but his pleas were drowned out by Lawdmot and his followers. They smelled blood.

In the next inning Dandyboy hit a hard grounder between third and shortstop. Meglamike raced over, stopped the ball, turned, threw to first base and beat Dandyboy to the base. Why had not Dandyboy, so fleet of foot, beaten out that shot for a hit? Was he still thinking about his prior miscue? In the innings that followed, the Natleos continued to score runs, the Dalespringers continued to commit errors (eight in all), and finally at the end of three innings they were "mercied" by the ten-run rule. How humiliating, thought Dandyboy.

That night Dandyboy was inconsolable. He would not eat supper. He even took a shower without being asked. Dandyboy would not even play the video game he loved to play. He went to his bedroom. "What are we going to do," thought Dandyboy. "I wish I knew what to do" he said out loud. "If only Guardfather could tell me a story," he thought. "Guardfather knows a story for everything."

"I remember the time Guardfather, the famous Storymaster, told me about Joe D. Magico and the pinstripers and how they played for the joy of playing. And what about the Cityknicks with Dave Defense, Prince Bradley, The Jewel, Frazslick, and Ruler Reed. Remember how they won the championship against the Celts of Bosstown and the Left Coast Lakers? If only he would come and tell me a story."

Miraculously, Storymaster, the Guardfather of Dandyboy, appeared and sat on the bed next to him.

"What is it Dandyboy?" asked Storymaster, "Why do you look so glum? How come you showered?"

"I stunk today, Guardfather."

"Is that why you showered?" responded Storymaster.

"Very funny, you know what I mean," said Dandyboy. "I made two errors, I didn't run to first base as fast as I could, I let my teammates down, especially Double A, Dentistson, and Gregnevermoan. I feel awful. I think I'm going to quit playing baseball."

"Hold on, Dandyboy. One game does not a season make, as someone once said," replied the sagacious Storymaster. "Even the great Joe D. Magico made errors. Errors are part of the game. However, not running as fast as you could is something the great Joe D. would not do. Dandyboy, you must always run your fastest," continued Guardfather. "Dandyboy, before you quit, let me tell you a story of someone who could have quit and did not and maybe you will think again before you do."

"Dandyboy, let me tell you the story of the payback, for you will learn from this story that no boy can wish for anything better than the payback.

"Four friends went to school together. They were studying to be officers in the British army. One was there in order to satisfy his father's wishes, for his father had been a great general and dreamed of glory for his son, but the son had no love for the army. At this time Britain was at war in Africa. Upon graduation from the military school the boy who had no love for the army chose not to accept his commission.

"The three others thought him a coward as did the girl who thought she loved him. As was the custom of the day each gave the young boy a white feather. The white feather was the sign of disgrace and one who wished to redeem himself had to perform an act of heroism that would require the giver of the white feather to accept it back. This was the 'payback.'

"The three who remained in the Army went to war in Africa. The young man who did not love the Army followed them. He disguised himself so that no one would know who he was. With great courage and with much pain to himself, he had his skin scarred by a burning iron and then darkened his skin to give the appearance of a desert wanderer. He assumed the role of a silent fool who could not speak.

"One of the givers of the white feather, while leading a patrol, was overcome by the heat. His unshielded eyes were permanently damaged by the sun. He was blinded. Then his patrol was over run by the enemy. All were killed except him. He was left for dead. The young man who did not love the army found him and led him back to the main army base. He had fulfilled his first act of heroism.

"The young man who did not love the Army searched out his remaining two friends. They had been captured and were in a prison with hundreds of others. The final act of bravery occurred when he broke into prison and led a revolt that freed his friends and led to the conquest of the enemy.

"When the girl who loved the boy who did not love the army found out about his bravery she asked for the white feather back. The boy who did not love the army was very happy for he loved the girl and now he had his girl and he had gotten the payback. So Dandyboy, do not despair. You, too, can have the payback. Your task is easier for all you have to do is win three games and you don't have to go to Africa, or scar your face."

"Thank you, Storymaster," said Dandyboy. "Do you think I can get the payback?"

"One other thing, Dandyboy," reminded Storymaster. "Payback does no come to all who want it. Even the bravest who try their hardest don't always get it and only the luckiest succeed."

"I want to try anyway," replied Dandyboy, "even if I do not get the payback."

Dandyboy fell asleep dreaming of the payback. When he awoke he found an envelope on his bed. "What is this?" Dandyboy murmured. "Oh my goodness," he shouted, "there are three white feathers in the envelope."

In the days that followed the Dalespringers practiced very hard. They were not the carefree group they usually were. To win the championship of Galaxy I, they would have to beat the winner of the loser's bracket and then beat Natleos twice. No easy task when you remember that they did not score a run against Natleos.

As it turned out the Stars of the North were to be their opponents in the loser's bracket championship. The game was scheduled for Saturday.

When the day arrived Dandyboy was chosen to pitch. "Was Storymaster right," thought Dandyboy. "Would he have a chance for payback? Could he payback Double A and Gregnevermoan and Dentistson?"

Before the game Coach Macramike walked over to Dandyboy. "Dandyboy," he announced, "you are to be our pitcher today.

Throw the ball that curves for the Stars of the North are the hitters of long balls and they like the pitch with fire."

Dandyboy replied, "Okay coach, I will throw the ball that curves." He did not tell Coach Macramike about the visit from Storymaster and the payback.

Coach Macramike then said, "Manager Jim Aged did not want you to pitch. He wanted Double A, but I said, 'Dandyboy will do it for us,' so don't let me down."

Dandyboy felt the panic seize him. Another one has put the pressure on me. Maybe I should tell Coach I don't feel well, that my arm hurts. But then he remembered Storymaster's words, "Only the most brave feel the rewards of payback."

In the first inning Dandyboy threw the ball that curves and fooled some of the batters. But often the ball would not curve and the ball was struck. Gregnevermoan stopped a ball in the middle and threw out the runner at first. One batter was fooled by the ball that curves and popped up a ball that Dandyboy ran back to catch and the inning was over.

For the Stars of the North, Bigman was pitching. He had lost to the Dalespringers in the last game but only because Double A was so outstanding. The other Dalespringers had much difficulty in hitting the ball. Bigman threw smoke and he threw with the arm from the south. In the first inning for the Dalespringers three batters reached bases but no run would score. Bigman was wild and Dandyboy walked. He had not received a strike from Bigman in three times that he went to bat.

In the second inning the ball that curves would not. Dandyboy seemed to be in trouble. The mighty hitters from the Stars of the North could see that the ball would hang and they would hit it. Zack of the Home Run hit a double and two others hit singles. The score was two to nothing and would have reached more if Dandyboy did not make two spectacular plays.

Bigman, who can hit the ball that leaves the park, hit a wicked shot that looked like it would decapitate Dandyboy. In the last possible moment, Dandyboy put up his glove and caught the ball and threw out Bigman who was running to first. With men still on base the next batter hit a low line drive that Dandyboy dove for and caught before it hit the ground for the final out. Dandyboy was trying his hardest but he recalled the words of Storymaster, "Not all who try their hardest get the payback." Dandyboy wondered if he would be lucky enough to get the payback.

The Dalespringers in their half of the second inning could not get anything going. Bigman seemed to get stronger with each pitch. He blazed the ball by the Dalespringers and when the ball was struck it seemed destined to end up in the fielder's glove. The coaches felt snakebit.

Coach Macramike shouted, "What is happening? It's like the ball has eyes. What is going on?" Then in order to inspire his troops, Macramike said, "Dalespringers, don't despair. Our turn will come. The ball will soon elude the Stars of the North."

In the next inning it appeared as if Dandyboy was inspired by Coach Macramike. He began to throw the ball that curves. In one fine display of pitching, Dandyboy fooled Zack of the Home Run on three pitches and struck him out. The next batter was Twoton, the catcher of the Stars of the North. He was a powerfully built boy, the prototype of the catcher of yesteryear. He could be dangerous with the bat. Dandyboy had to be careful with his pitches. The first pitch was the ball that curves and Twoton swung and missed. Dandyboy looked at his catcher Dentistson for the sign of what to pitch. He shook off the first sign and nodded his head to signal the acceptance of the catcher's suggestion. It looked like the ball that curves, but it didn't. Twoton was waiting but perhaps was a little too anxious. He smashed into the ball and it rose in flight and sailed out of the park in left field. The umpire, however, signaled that the ball was foul. Dandyboy had been lucky. After throwing a pitch that was clearly outside the strike zone, Dandyboy returned to his famous pitch and struck out Twoton.

Dandyboy breathed a sigh of relief. Too soon, however, for the next batter was the center fielder and relief pitcher for the Stars of the North, a hitter of singles who managed to strike one of Dandyboy's baseballs just right and it sailed over Double A's head for a home run. Dandyboy learned another lesson, don't take the light hitter too lightly. The inning ended with a fly out to the left fielder.

In the third inning the first two hitters at bat for the Dalespringers made outs. The Dalespringers were not only without a run in the last two games but they were also without a hit in this game. Coach Macramike was concerned that he had made a mistake to pitch Dandyboy and not Double A. Manager Jim Aged began to pace the dugout. He too wondered why Macramike had talked him into using Dandyboy.

"Tell me, Macramike, what were you thinking when you put Dandyboy on the mound?" whispered Jim Aged.

"Relax, Jim," replied Macramike, "Dandy's a winner, he'll come through."

Although they said nothing to him, Dandyboy began to sense their frustration. As he walked to the plate to take his turn at bat, Dandyboy sought within himself the strength to prevail. "I must lead this team to victory," he whispered. "Please Bigman, throw me a pitch to hit and I will show my teammates that we are not without hope. Guardfather, make Bigman throw me a strike," Dandyboy mumbled to himself.

On the first pitch from Bigman, the first strike he had thrown Dandyboy in two games, Dandyboy lined a shot into left field for a single. The next batter, Totalpaul, a usually potent hitter, who had not had a great Galaxy tournament, hit a double to right field. Dandyboy raced to third base. Pavloga, the Dalespringer's second baseman stroked a single and Dandyboy scored.

Friendlyfan rose up, "Yes, we got a chance. Let's hear it for the team from the dale beyond the spring." A roar of approval followed: "Dalespringers! Dalespringers!"

There was still hope for the Dalespringers. At the end of three innings, the score was three to one in favor of the Stars of the North.

In the fourth inning, the Stars of the North scored another run, the result of a misplay by the Dalespringers. Dandyboy struck out the first batter and the bail that curves was thrown with perfection. The next batter hit a slow ground ball to Fetchthrow, the third baseman.. It appeared to be an easy out but the ball got stuck in the webbing of Fetchthrow's glove. He tried to pull the ball out so that he could throw out the runner. When he did manage to do so, he rushed the throw, which sailed over the head of Totalpaul, the first baseman. The runner advanced to second base.

The next batter bunted the ball. It was struck very hard. Totalpaul ran in to get the ball. It went by him. First base was unprotected as the ball trickled toward Pavloga who was forced to retrieve the ball. Dandyboy, seeing first base unprotected, raced toward the base. Pavloga threw the ball to him but it was a bad throw and the ball raced behind Dandyboy. The runner from second scored and the bunter reached second base. The hope that emerged last inning seemed to be fleeting. Dandyboy was again faced with a challenge. Would he wilt? The look of concentration beamed from his face. His eyes were focused on the catcher. He seemed on a mission as he struck out the next two batters. The local fans were silent.

Friendlyfan stood up to lead cheers, "Let's go Dalespringers! Let's go Dalespringers!" No response. The crowd was sullen.

The Dalespringers had a bad fourth inning at bat. Bigman was seemingly unstoppable. Batters flailed at pitches. Coach Macramike was furious. "Why do you help Bigman? Why do you swing at bad pitches?" The batters slunk back to the dugout, their heads hung low. Were the Stars of the North really going to eliminate the Dalespringers?

In the top of the fifth inning, Dandyboy remained focused. He threw only four pitches as the Stars of the North went out. A pop up to Dentistson behind the plate retired the first batter. An easy ground ball back to Dandyboy created the second out. The final batter of the inning on the second pitch to him, hit the ball that curves softly up in the air right in front of the mound and Dandyboy caught it for the final out.

When the Dalespringers returned to the dugout, Dandyboy jumped up and shouted to his teammates, "This is our inning, believe me, I know it. Everybody tries a little harder," he exhorted them.

"Yeah," said Dentistson, "Dandyboy is the only one working hard, let's get them now!!"

Dandyboy was thankful for Dentistson's words. He needed everyone to help if he was to get the payback.

The bottom of the fifth inning started off well for the Dalespringers. The first two batters walked. Bigman seemed angry. He could not get control of the heat. His balls sailed all over the place and the batters, instead of flailing at the balls, remained patient. Coach Macramike's words were planted in their minds. The next batter was Dentistson. He hit a grounder between second and short that the second baseman knocked down but he had no play and the bases were loaded.

Guess who stepped up to the plate? You guessed it, Double A, the hero of game one against Bigman. The coach of the Stars of the North, Protestal, walked out to speak to Bigman.

When time was called, the fans of the Dalespringers were shouting with joy and cheering for Double A to hit the grandest of all slams.

"Double A, Double A," shouted Friendlyfan. This time the loyalists were excited.

"He can do it, Double A can do it," came the response from one fan.

"Double A did it before, he can do it again," came the chant.

Bigman, however, was not going to give Double A a good pitch to hit. As a matter of fact, with the count two balls and no strikes, he struck Double A in the arm with the ball. Double A was awarded first base and a run was forced in. Gregnevermoan was the next batter.

Coach Protestal called time out and signaled for his relief pitcher to come in. Bigman was moved to center field and the center fielder was called in to pitch. He, like Dandyboy, was a thrower of the ball that curved. On his first pitch Gregnevermoan tapped the ball that curves. It rolled toward third base and no one could field it fast enough to get a runner out. Another run scored. The score was now Stars of the North four, Dalespringers three.

Dandyboy was the next hitter. "Oh, Storymaster my Guardfather, could anything be more wished for than this, a chance to get the hit that wins the game," were the words he spoke to himself. "Can I rescue my team from defeat?"

The relief pitcher knew that he must pitch carefully to Dandyboy for Dandyboy was known to have the eye. He would not swing at the pitches that were bad. The pitcher also knew that four bad pitches would allow a run to score. His first pitch was a ball, as was the second. Normally a pitch following two balls was a strike, a hitter's pitch in the language of baseballers. Coach Macramike, however, wanted Dandyboy to accept the next pitch without swinging. It was a strike and Dandyboy appeared upset that he was required to accept the pitch without hitting.

Dandyboy walked out of the batter's box, "Why didn't coach let me hit that pitch?" mumbled Dandyboy.

Coach Macramike shouted into Dandyboy, "Come on Dandy, swing away, get a hit."

Dandyboy smiled. He could hear Friendlyfan shouting, "Win the game yourself Dandy. We know you can do it."

"Yeah," shouted the others.

On the next pitch, Dandyboy swung and struck the ball. It flew out into right field. Dentistson scored as did Double A. Gregnevermoan, however, rounded third and momentarily stopped before he tried to score. A perfect relay throw nailed him at home. But two runs had scored, the Dalespringers were now ahead five to four. Dandyboy's face was aglow with a smile as he stood on second base with a double. No more Dalespringer runs scored in the inning.

All that remained now for the Dalespringers to win was to get three outs before two runs scored. The first batter to face Dandyboy in the sixth inning was the shortstop. Dandyboy's pitch appeared to be guided by a computer. Each time as the batter swung, the ball eluded the bat and ended up in the mitt of Dentistson. One out by way of strikeout. On the first pitch to the next batter the ringing sounds of a hard-hit ball were heard. A single to center. Man on first base. The following batter bunted the ball to advance the runner and Fetchthrow fielded the ball perfectly, hesitated a moment and then threw the ball to second base. Too late, signaled the umpire. Runners on first and second, one out. Another attempted sacrifice was undertaken by the Stars of the North batter. Dandyboy pounced off the mound like a cat, picked up the ball, whirled, and threw to third base.

"Out" came the shout of the umpire on third base.

Two outs, runner on first and second. Friendlyfan and the fans of the Dalespringers rose to their feet shouting, "One more out! One more out!" There was bedlam.

Zack of the Home Run was the batter. Dandyboy wound up and threw the ball that curves. Zack lunged at the ball as it fell to the ground. Strike one. Dandyboy looked in to Dentistson for the signal. The fans were shouting "Dandyboy, throw the ball that curves!" Dandyboy threw. It was not the ball that curves. It is what Zack had hoped for. He smashed the ball into right field for a double and two runs scored. The Stars of the North now led by one run. Friendlyfan and his group of followers were silent.

Twoton rolled to the plate. He had fire in his eyes for Dandyboy had fooled him the time before. But Dandyboy had his number and made short work of him on three pitches.

The Dalespringers faced a true test. Can they rally once more to win this so-important game? There is a chance, for coming to bat in this inning will be Dentistson, Double A and Gregnevermoan. There is silence in the dugout. Coach Macramike calls the boys together.

"This is it Dalespringers. Let's see what you are made of. Let's get this one for Dandyboy who has played so hard. Let's do it!"

The boys hear the words and shout out their support. But can we do it? think so many of them.

Dentistson raised the hopes of everyone when be smacked a line drive into center field. Double A comes to bat. Could you ask for a better chance? The most powerful batter at the plate with the tying run on base. "Go Double A!" comes the cheering from the fans.

Double A works the count to two balls and one strike. Will Coach Macramike let Double A swing? ponder the loyal followers of the Dalespringers? The answer came quickly as Double A unfolded his arms and smacked the pitch. The ball sails skyward destined to clear the fence for a homerun. The fans are shouting with joy for a home run will produce the two tallies required to win.

Too soon are their cheers, for Bigman, now playing center field races to the fence and as the ball is about to leave the ballpark he leaps and pulls it in. The victory of the Dalespringers is averted and the Stars of the North are two outs away from the championship. A sense of gloom starts to settle on the fans of the home team.

Gregnevermoan is the batter. He erupts on the first pitch. When the ball is retrieved by the Stars of the North, he has a single. Dentistson is standing on second base and Gregnevermoan is stationed at first base.

Dandyboy puts on his batting helmet and selects the bat that has already produced two hits today. "Storymaster, I know you gave me the one chance to be heroic and get the payback. Is it too much to ask for the chance again? Let my bat swing true," Dandyboy recites to himself.

"Batter up," the umpire shouts. Dandyboy strides to the plate. The crowd is standing. The first pitch gets away from the catcher and Dentistson goes to third base and Gregnevermoan reaches second base. The relief pitcher's next delivery is swung on by Dandyboy. His swing is true. The ball eludes the shortstop and the third baseman and rolls to the fence in left field. Dentistson and Gregnevermoan score. Dandyboy has done it again. The Dalespringers win.

Wait! The coach of the Stars of the North Protestal refuses to concede victory. The coach of the Stars runs out on the field. "Protest! Protest!" shouts Protestal.

"What is it coach, another protest?" inquires the head umpire.

"Yup, Dandyboy never ran to first base," he retorted.

"That's crazy Protestal, I saw him run to first base, but I'll check it with the first base umpire," is the reply.

The fans are appalled. How could a coach mar a game so valiantly played by both sides? After deliberating over the appeal, the umpires dismiss it as frivolous. The safe sign is flashed. The Dalespringers win.

That night as Dandyboy sat on his bed remembering the day, he is visited by Storymaster. "Did you hear about our game, Guardfather?" asks Dandyboy.

"Some of it, but tell me what happened Dandyboy" said Storymaster.

"I pitched and I had three hits and I knocked in four runs and in the last inning I had the hit that scored the winning runs," replies Dandyboy.

"That is great, you were most heroic Dandyboy"

"Does this mean that I have the payback now?"

"Let me ask you this, Dandyboy, can you feel that you have had the payback before you beat the Natleos? It is up to you," said Storymaster.

"I guess not," said Dandyboy, "but it sure felt like a little payback today."

"You are right" said Storymaster as he is ready to leave. "It is a little payback; maybe one feather's worth," he says as he reaches out to accept one white feather from Dandyboy.

Finally the day that everyone had waited for had come. The championship round would begin. The Dalespringers, winners of the loser's bracket would need two victories to claim the Galaxy I Championship. The Natleos were a confident group. They had devastated the Dalespringers in the first game, a "mercy game" called after three innings because of the ten-run rule. They knew it would end today.

It was a steaming hot day. The heat of yesterday persisted.

Fans sought the shelter of the shade. The Dalespringers' fans disdained the comfort of the trees that offered an escape from the rays of the sun. They had come to cheer their team on and accepted the heat with dignity as they lined the field on the side designated for the Dalespringers. The Dalespringers were the home team.

During the warm up the Dalespringers displayed an unusual calm. It was a determined group of players. Unlike the rowdy and boisterous Natleos, they were quiet, subdued, and confident, the contrast was eerie.

On the Natleo's side Reyjose was joking with Efrespro. "Hey man, we can really celebrate tonight," he shouted.

"Yeah, I feel real strong today, those Dalespringers look real scared."

'"Can you blame them," laughed Bucklehomer as he flexed his muscles. "Look who's pitching for us."

Laughter from the Natleos team erupted after the remark.

Dandyboy nervously paced the sideline waiting for the contest to commence. He cheered on his teammates urging them to play hard.

"Dentistson, you got to hit today and you, Double A, just throw the fire," he suggested.

"We'll get hits today, I feel it," chimed in Gregnevermoan

Dandyboy would neither throw the ball that curved nor wear the armor of the catcher. Coach Macramike wanted him rested and placed in the field at center.

Dandyboy thought to himself, "We can win." His teammate from league play, Terrifictom, was back from his trip. He would play today. Dandyboy murmured, "Terrifictom will help me with the payback, he's my friend." Terrifictom would guard the base known as third. He was terrific at that place. More importantly, Terrifictom had a mighty bat. The ball seemed to jump off the metal when he swung and with his fleet feet he would run the paths of the bases like Mercury. Only Dandyboy was faster.

The thrower of fire, Double A would pitch against Meglamike. The Natleos felt invincible for Meglamike had not lost a pitching duel and after all Reyjose had silenced the bats of the opposition in the earlier game. How could they hit Meglamike, who throws fire and the ball that curved? The smirks on the faces of Meglamike's teammates were apparent. Would this arouse the anger of the Dalespringers?

It sure seemed to. Double A, in a display of both heat and control, struck out Reyjose and Meglamike in their first at bats. Meglamike came roaring back in his turn at pitching. Although the side was retired in order, the Dalespringers seemed to gain a sense of confidence. Meglamike and his ball of fire were not unhittable. Each batter made sound contact with the ball. Even though each of the batters had not gained a base when he returned to the dugout, his enthusiasm was evident. "Come on guys, we can hit this guy," was the familiar statement of each of the returning batters.

In the second inning, Double A lost his sense of direction. The ball could not find the zone for strikes. Double A, after retiring the first two batters, walked four Natleos in a row. A run was scored. The fans of the Natleos, a boisterous group at best, were relentless in their jeers and taunts.

"These guys are terrible, we can crush them," shouts came crashing down on the Dalespringers.

Finally Double A got the last batter to ground out.

When the Dalespringers came to bat, Terrifictom was the first hitter. He had not been in the competition and many wondered what he would do. Dandyboy thought he was a powerful batter but some fans wondered about Coach Macramike's choice to bat his friend.

"How come Terrifictom is batting cleanup," said one fan.

"I don't know," was the response from another follower of the game. "He sure doesn't look ready to me."

Well, as if it were delivered from the lips of the oracle at Delphi, the prediction came through. Terrifictom struck out. He did manage to hit two long foul balls prior to his missed swing, but nevertheless it was an out. The Dalespringers desperately needed a run, or at the very least a hit.

Dandyboy selected his bat and went to the plate. "I've got to get a hit," he murmured to Totalpaul.

"You will Dandyboy," Totalpaul responded. "You are in the zone." To be in the zone is what every hitter dreams of. You must take advantage of it for the zone does not come very often and to some it never comes. Dandyboy remembered what Storymaster had told him. "The great Joe D. Magico was in the zone for 56 days," Storymaster related to Dandyboy. "He was in the zone longer than any other baseballer."

Dandyboy struck the first pitch of Meglamike. The ball traveled on the ground between third and shortstop, the same place where Dandyboy had hit the ball in the first game against the Natleos. Unlike the ill-fated first game, Dandyboy did not dally. His legs exploded like rockets as he fled from home to first.

"No one will throw me out today," Dandyboy said as he thought of the payback. When the play ended, Dandyboy was on first base with the first hit off of Meglamike. A cheer rose up from the Dalespringer fans. They had so little to cheer about in the first game. A hit became a symbol of something good even though they were losing one to nothing.

Totalpaul picked up his bat and strode excitedly to the batter's box. He too wanted a hit so badly that he could hardly wait for the chance. And sure enough, Totalpaul came through with a line drive to center field. The Dalespringers seemed on their way. But wait a minute. For what seemed like the beginning of a roll ended in a mild disaster.

Coach Macramike wanting his Dalespringers to score a run, urged Dandyboy to try for third base on Totalpaul's single. Arms moving, Coach Macramike yelled, "Run, Dandy, run! Come to me"

Unfortunately, Reyjose was charging the ball and in a graceful display scooped up the ball and fired it directly to third base. Dandyboy, flying around second base in response to Coach Macramike's request, could not retreat to the safety of second bane. He was out at third base. What started out so promising ended with Meglamike getting two outs before a run could be scored.

In the top of the third inning, Double A got Reyjose and the next batter to strike out. Meglamike then hit a line drive to center field. Before Dandyboy could retrieve it and return it to the infield, Meglamike was standing safely on the bag at second. Efrespro singled. The following hitter, the catcher, stroked a single to right field and Meglamike raced home with run number two for the Natleos. Double A then managed to shut the door and not allow any more runs, but the score was two to nothing.

In the stands behind the Dalespringer's dugout you could hear the fans' worries. "When are the guys going to score a run?"

"Yeah, I mean, like, what's happening?"

"They don't have the hitters in the right order," said an angry fan.

"Come on fans, we can't get down on the boys or the coach," responded an enlightened observer.

With that final comment, the fans cheered loudly in support of the boys and in response to the boisterous jeers of the Natleo's fans, hopeful their chant would drown out the taunts.

If ever the Dalespringers were going to score it would have

to come now. The power of the batting order was scheduled to bat. Dentistson, still smarting over the loss to the Natleos, was determined to get a hit. On a one and one pitch he laced a rope into center field and raced swiftly to first. His arm raised triumphantly as he stood on the bag. Double A followed with a single to left. There was a momentary silence when Terrifictom strode to the plate. He could sense the fans' concern in light of his absence from earlier games and his last strikeout. He wasted little time in proving to the crowd that Coach Macramike was correct in batting him fourth. A wicked shot rolled out to the fence. Dentistson scored from second, Double A ended up on third as Terrifictom had an R.B.I. double to his credit. An eruption of noise came thundering down from the Dalespringer loyals.

"I knew we could do it," shouted a previously disillusioned fan. Their team had scored. It was now two to one.

Gregnevermoan was the batter. After fouling off two of Meglamike's fast balls, the third strike was called by the Umpire.

"You're blind, Ump," came the response of a fan. "Give us a break."

The call was heatedly disputed by the fans, but Gregnevermoan, true to his name, raised nary a protest. The Natleo fans became uncontrollable, hurling unfair epitaphs at the players. Dandyboy picked up his white steel bat that had clubbed out four straight hits and marched off to face the offerings of Meglamike.

Meglamike roared back and hurled a flaming ball of fire. The umpire signaled strike one. Again a protest by the fans but no indication from Dandyboy that he disputed the umpire. The next offering from Meglamike was another fireball. Dandyboy uncocked his wrists, his hips rotated properly, the bat met the ball sending it over the left fielder's head. Double A scored, Terrifictom raced around third and scored. Dandyboy rested on second thrilled by the roar of the crowd as they rose to their feet to honor the latest heroics of Dandyboy. Silence fell over the Natleos and their fans. They had never been behind before. No further damage was caused and the third inning ended with the score Dalespringers three, Natleos two.

In the fourth inning, Meglamike came to bat. He hit a hard grounder close to the third base line. It looked like it would surely go through the infield for a double. But Terrifictom, who had been positioned here because of his ability, backhanded the ball, spun around, and gunned out Meglamike at first. It was truly a play of beauty. Again, the spontaneous eruption of the fans cheering in appreciation of a great play came forth from the Dalespringers side of the field.

"Way to go, Terrifictom, way to go," beckoned Friendlyfan.

"Did you see that play? That was major league," said one enthusiast to another.

The inning ended with no runs scored.

The Dalespringers were equally silent in their half of the fourth. The fifth inning was a repeat of the fourth. The pitchers Double A and Meglamike seemed to gain strength with each pitch. The fielders too played at a great level of intensity. Out after out occurred. The tension was overwhelming. Fans mumbled to one another, "Can one run hold up?", "Who would weaken first?", "Is Double A strong enough to continue?"

Double A walked to the mound to start the last inning. Whether he could get three outs and the victory was foremost in his thoughts. He seemed to be in control and the first batter fell victim to his blazing ball of fire.

"Two more outs to go!" shouted a fan.

The next batter after receiving two bad pitches topped the next pitch. It rolled to the mound and Double A picked it up and threw out the runner at first. *Two outs.* The noise became deafening. Could the Dalespringers really beat the Untouchable Natleos?

The cheering may have started too soon. Double A with his burst of fire could not find the plate. Two Natleos walked. The next batter was Reyjose. He was very fast. On a slow hit ball to first base he raced passed the outstretched arm of Totalpaul and was safe. Coming to bat was Meglamike, truly a superstar of the Galaxy. He too proved to the fans why all coaches looked at him with awe. Meglamike stroked a single to left field and two runs scored. The Natleos had taken the lead. Their fans, silent for so long, burst out with boisterous bellowing.

"'Yeah! Meglamike you're the best, way to go," roared Lawdmot.

"They're going to quit now—those Dalespringers have no heart," yelled another Natleo fan.

Meglamike waved to the crowd his acknowledgment of their approval.

It looked like a sad ending for the gallant effort of the Dalespringers. Double A signaled that his arm was sore and Gregnevermoan was called in to pitch. It was not an enviable position to be in. There were two Natleos on base and the ever-dangerous Efrespo was to be the batter. Gregnevermoan is a thrower of heat but on occasion can throw the ball that curved. His first pitch was of heat and Efrespo on the coach's instruction did not swing.

"Strike one," shouted the umpire.

The next offering was foul. The ball curved off as it sailed to the outfield. Dandyboy, who was now playing shortstop, walked over to Gregnevermoan.

"Don't give him anything good on this pitch and then throw him the ball that curves," was his advice.

"Okay, Dandyboy. Don't worry, I've got it under control," was Gregnevermoan's response.

On the next pitch, a ball of heat, Efrespo did not swing as the position of the ball was too close to him. The umpire signaled it was a ball. Gregnevermoan then threw the ball that curves. Efrespo, obviously fooled by the pitch, started to swing and then tried to check it. It was too late and the umpire flashed the "out" sign. Gregnevermoan had stopped the Natleos from scoring. Nevertheless, the Dalespringers were behind four to three.

Meglamike ran out to the mound. He was pumped up and could sense the victory that would make his team the Galaxy I champions. He was a great competitor who faced up to challenge with much courage. Meglamike often led the team to victory. Once again he seemed on the verge of doing it. But the Dalespringers refused to die easily.

Double A in hope of redemption, led off with a single that was followed by an out when Terrifictom's fly ball to center was caught by Reyjose. Gregnevermoan then walked and Dandyboy came to bat. Fans started shouting, "Come on Dandy, we need a hit!"

Was it possible he could get another hit? The question was quickly answered when Dandyboy's bat struck the ball sending a lazy grounder to the shortstop. For some reason, Double A stopped midway between second and third. The maneuver confused the shortstop who could have easily thrown to second and then back to first for a double play. When the shortstop regained his composure, his only option was to throw to third base. The ball arrived before Double A, so the second out occurred.

When the diminutive left fielder Carmbren came to bat, Gregnevermoan was on second base and Dandyboy was on first. There were two outs and if a run did not score the Dalespringers would be through.

Meglamike's first pitch got away from the catcher and

Gregnevermoan scooted to third base and Dandyboy advanced to second. The noise at the arena was ear shattering. The Natleos yelling for the third out, the Dalespringers urging Carmbren to strike the ball squarely. Meglamike wound up and threw. Carmbren swung and hit the ball. It was looping over the second baseman's head. The ball fell in front of the right fielder. Gregnevermoan easily scored. Dandyboy raced past third base and was flying toward home plate with the potential winning run. The right fielder threw the ball toward the catcher, Dandyboy slid and rolled over the plate before the catcher could tag him. The Dalespringers won!

It was a most joyous moment for Dandyboy and the Dalespringers. The game had been a gallant effort by both teams. The play was of the highest caliber. The Dalespringers had done what many had thought impossible. They could now approach the final game with renewed vigor and with renewed confidence.

It was clear that the emotions of the game had drained the participants for there was not a great deal of celebrating. Coach Macramike praised the boys but warned against overconfidence, "Boys, it doesn't mean anything unless we win Tuesday."

Dandyboy went home. As he sat on his bed he said to Storymaster, "I think I know what the payback is."

"Not yet my friend," warned Storymaster, "for now not only do you seek the payback but so does Meglamike and the Natleos."

"Oh, that is true, Storymaster," replied Dandyboy. "But can two people have payback?"

"I don't think so, when two people seek the same payback, only the bravest most dedicated, and most lucky can find true payback," responded Storymaster.

"Go to bed now, rest up for the final game. You have been

most courageous but you will need much energy to continue" Storymaster said as he left the room.

Storymaster stuck his head back in, "Remember, Dandyboy, the secret is to try your hardest, then you can look any boy in the eye, even if you don't get the payback."

The final game, the game to decide the Galaxy I Championship was played on the night of Tuesday. Prior to the game a day of rest and thought had been granted to the contestants. Dandyboy had spent the day before the game thinking about remaining in the zone. He polished the bat that had produced the hits that led to victory. He wondered where he would play this final game. Would he be called upon to throw the ball that curved or would he wear the suit of armor.

"Oh, great Guardfather, don't let me embarrass myself, let me be brave and make me try my hardest," he said to himself just prior to the moment of sleep.

On the night of the game it was decided by Coach Macramike that Gregnevermoan would pitch. Dentistson was still of a sore arm and Dandyboy had pitched on Saturday. Both could be called upon if Gregnevermoan faltered. The Natleos decided to use Reyjose, the lefty who had fooled the Dalespringers so badly in the game he pitched against them. He was quite cocky. His pitches curved and he seldom walked a batter. On the other side of the field the Dalespringers were confident that they could hit Reyjose. Coach Macramike told them to be patient and step up in the batter's box so that they could hit the ball that curves before it breaks.

As the game was about to begin, the fans from both sides rose to cheer the participants. The Natleos, usually an unruly, boisterous crowd was somewhat subdued. It probably reflected their surprise at having lost the last game. Nevertheless they were there to urge their team on. The Dalespringers' followers were excited but controlled in their enthusiasm.

Gregnevermoan was the lead-off batter and he quickly stroked a single off of Reyjose. Dentistson followed with a hard-hit ball on the ground that looked like it would go through for a hit. Miraculously Meglamike ran the ball down and threw to second to force out Gregnevermoan. It was clear that Meglamike was going to try his hardest.

Double A, the next batter, hit a fly ball to left field which was caught. The Dalespringers were excited about hitting Reyjose, who had not allowed very much activity in the first game. Terrifictom, who followed Double A, wasted no time in showing the faithful why he was the number four hitter as he laced a double to left. Dentistson raced to third but was held up by Coach Macramike.

Dandyboy picked up the freshly polished bat and swung it a few times. Be then signaled to the umpire that he was ready. Reyjose threw the ball that curves. It appeared to fool Dandyboy but he managed to make contact with the ball. It headed out to left field but at the last moment curved foul. Strike one. The next pitch was a ball that curved but it zoomed low and outside. Ball one. Reyjose looked to the catcher for a sign. He shook off one sign. Then he stretched and threw. It was not the pitch that curves but a high hard one. Dandyboy was ready. He swung the bat perfectly. The ball rebounded off the metal and soared deep to right field. It sailed over the head of the right fielder. Dentistson scored. Terrifictom scored. Dandyboy ended up on third base with a triple. The Dalespringer fans were on their feet. They were shouting "Dandyboy! Dandyboy!"

Coach Macramike patted him on the back. Dandyboy knew this was just the beginning, the game had only started. On the next pitch the ball bounced away from the catcher and Dandyboy scooted home. Three runs had scored.

The Natleos seemed stunned. In their half of the inning they went out one, two, three. In the next half inning the defense of the Natleos faltered and Totalpaul and Carmbren scored. Two more runs now were added to the three scored in the first inning. The Natleos in their half of the inning got two hits off of Gregnevermoan but could not score a run.

In the third inning the Dalespringers could not produce a run. The Natleos seemed to regroup in their half of the inning. Gregnevermoan walked the first batter he faced. Then the right fielder got a single. The next batter grounded out but the two runners advanced to second and third. Reyjose was now the batter. He tried to bunt the first pitch but fouled it off. Gregnevermoan then struck him out on two balls of fire.

Meglamike came to the plate. He was a dangerous hitter. He was especially competitive when runners were on base. He swung and missed on the first pitch. The next pitch by Gregnevermoan hung up too high. Meglamike was all over it and lined a double to left field. Carmbren's throw to second was bad and Meglamike raced toward third. Totalpaul, who was backing up the second baseman, misplayed the ball and Meglamike raced home to score.

It was now five to three and the Natleo fans were jubilant. The noise was deafening. The Dalespringers' fans were worried the boys would wilt. Their fears were short lived as Gregnevermoan got Efrespro to fly out to Double A in center field.

The tempo slowed down in the fourth inning as the Dalespringers could produce nary a run and nary a hit. The Natleos were a little more successful. A hit and an error after two outs left runners on first and third. While pitching to the next batter, Gregnevermoan threw a ball that bounced in front of the plate and rolled past Dandyboy. As he raced to retrieve it the runner from third broke for home. Alertly Gregnevermoan charged in toward the plate. Dandyboy recovered the ball and pitched it to Gregnevermoan covering the plate. The runner slid to avoid the tag but he was too late. Gregnevermoan slapped the ball on him and the umpire flashed the familiar "out" sign. The Dalespringers had avoided a run being scored by the Natleos and the inning ended.

In the top of the fifth inning, Coach Macramike called the team together.

"Boys, we need some runs. Gregnevermoan is pitching his heart out. Let's get cracking and swing those bats," he implored.

"Yeah, let's get this one for Gregnevermoan, he never complains and we got to help him," responded the boys in unison.

Double A came through with a single to center and Terrifictom followed with his second hit, a single to left. Dandyboy slid his bat from the bat rack. As he placed his helmet on his head he thought, "Can I do it again?"

Reyjose remembered Dandyboy's triple in the first inning. He was not going to give Dandyboy anything too good. His first pitch was outside. On the next one Dandyboy was a little too anxious and pulled the ball foul. Reyjose threw the ball that curves to Dandyboy, who did not swing. He thought it would be ball two.

The umpire however saw it differently and shouted, "Strike two."

Reyjose was convinced that he could get the strikeout with the ball that curves. Dandyboy anticipated that it would be a ball that curves. He stepped forward in the batter's box. Sure enough Reyjose threw the pitch that was expected and Dandyboy hit a high fly ball to left field. Bucklehomer expecting the ball to fall short took two steps in. He suddenly realized that the ball was going deeper and at the last moment leaped to catch the ball. He managed to get his glove on the ball but it bounced out. Two runs scored as Dandyboy raced to third base with his second triple. Totalpaul hit the first pitch thrown by Reyjose for a single and Dandyboy trotted home. The Dalespringer's fans were shouting with glee as silence fell on the Natleos' section of the field.

Time was called and Reyjose was replaced as the pitcher for the Natleos. Efrespro was called in. He struck out Carmbren but the damage had been done. The Dalespringers now led eight to three. In the bottom of the fifth inning, Meglamike continued his hitting streak. He would not say die. Then Efrespro followed with a towering home run over the center field fence and the score was now eight to five. Gregnevermoan struck out the catcher before walking two batters. The inning finally ended with a strike out and a ground out third to first.

In the sixth inning the Dalespringers could not muster the power to produce a run. They entered the last inning leading by three runs. Coming up for the Natleos would be the number eight batter, the number nine batter, and the lead off hitter. If Gregnevermoan could get them out it would be all over. If not he would face Reyjose, usually a hard out, Meglamike who was on a tear, and Efrespro who hit the home run last at bat.

Coach Macramike huddled the boys together. "Boys, this is it, all we need is three out. and we win the Galaxy I championship. I know you want it. Go out there and do it."

This time there was no shouting. The players emerged from the dugout with a look of determination, with the quiet confidence so often apparent in true champions.

As Dandyboy moved toward his position behind the plate, Coach Macramike called him over. "Dandyboy, I'm counting on you to keep Gregnevermoan focused and calm. Give him a good target and let me know if you think something is wrong," the coach said.

"Coach, don't worry, Gregnevermoan looks sharp, we won't let this get away, besides, I want the payback," said Dandyboy as he put on his mask and ran behind the plate.

"What did you say, Dandyboy? You want what?" the coach shouted.

Dandyboy smiled to himself but ignored the coach's question. He would tell the coach all about it after the game.

Gregnevermoan threw his warmup pitches and then the number eight batter stepped to the plate. Dandyboy suspected a bunt especially after the batter kept looking at the coach at third base. Sure enough, on Gregnevermoan's first pitch the batter turned in the box and bunted the ball out in front of the plate. Dandyboy pounced on it like a cat and threw the ball to Totalpaul at first base. The runner was out by a mile. "One out," signaled Dandyboy.

A pinch hitter came to bat in place of the number nine hitter. He was a big kid who could hit the ball out of the park if he caught it. Dandyboy knew him. He called time out and walked out tot he mound to talk to Gregnevermoan.

"Greg, throw him two pitches that curve and then you'll throw the heat but it has to be inside," warned Dandyboy.

"Okay, Dandy, whatever you say," replied Gregnevermoan.

The first pitch broke down and away from the batter. His vicious awing missed the ball but the wind created gave everyone a scare. Gregnevermoan followed with the same pitch and again the rip of the bat failed. "Strike two." Dandyboy gave the sign for the heat and positioned himself to the inside of the batter. Gregnevermoan responded with the perfect pitch and the muscular lad struck out.

"Two outs," yelled Dandyboy.

Gregnevermoan and the Dalespringers were one out away from victory. The batter was the lead-off hitter. He had been unsuccessful in his previous at bats. But Gregnevermoan, after having delivered three perfect pitches to the previous batter, now could not find the plate. The batter walked. The Natleo fans, seeing a glimmer of hope, started their chanting and taunting in hopes of rattling Gregnevermoan.

The batter was Reyjose. Dandyboy wanted to be sure that Gregnevermoan knew who the next batter would be if Reyjose got on base. He signaled time out and ran out to the mound.

"Greg, listen. You got to get the ball over. Let Reyjose hit the ball. I promise you we'll get him out," implored Dandyboy.

"Yeah, Dandy, I just got a little careless with the other guy. I'm alright now," said Gregnevermoan.

"Okay, Greg, remember we don't want to face Meglamike or Efrespro again, right?"

"Right Dandyboy."

Dandyboy felt that Reyjose would take a pitch because the Natleos coach hoped that he would walk. Dandyboy signaled for a pitch straight down the middle. Sure enough Reyjose took the pitch and the umpire shouted, "Strike!" A cheer went up from the faithful fans of the Dalespringers. Dandyboy thought that Reyjose would not take the next pitch so he called for the ball that curved. Gregnevermoan threw the pitch, Reyjose swung and topped the pitch. The ball rolled out to Gregnevermoan. He fielded the ball and threw it to Totalpaul for the final out.

The Dalespringers win! The Dalespringers win!

"Do you believe in miracles," shouted Dalespringer fans.

In the meantime the Dalespringers, in their joyous moment of victory, mobbed the mound, the players tolling over one another. There was much in the way of festivities. The trophy was presented to the team. Some of the players were interviewed by the newspaper. Dandyboy was selected to speak to the television reporter. It was a momentous occasion, one that would be hard to forget.

After the players from each team shook hands. Dandyboy - then sat on the bench to take off his baseball shoes, Storymaster, his Guardfather, came over.

"Well, Dandyboy, how does it feel to be a hero, to get the payback," asked Storymaster.

"I'm no hero, Storymaster. When a team wins, everyone is a hero," answered Dandyboy.

"Yes, but what about the payback."

"You know Storymaster, I thought that the payback was the most important thing until I learned that the payback does not come to everyone. Look at Meglamike, he tried his hardest, why didn't he get the payback? Then I realized that the payback feels good, but the most important thing is to try your best then even if you don't get the payback, you can still feel good."

"Dandyboy, I'm proud of you. You learned a lot in these few days. You learned not to quit, you learned that the most important thing in life is to try your best. Remember that always," advised Storymaster. Storymaster as he rose to leave picked up the two white feathers and slapped a high five with Dandyboy.

"Later," both said.

DANDYBOY
AND THE SHOT
Another Fable

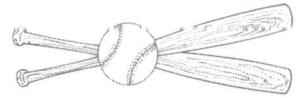

People knew about him from the time he was five. Could you expect anything different from a boy whose first word was not "mommy," not "daddy," but "ball"?

Dandyboy could dribble a basketball with both hands before he learned to tie his shoes. His coaches could not believe how he instinctively shot the ball with that perfect flick of the wrist. His anticipation and understanding of the game were uncanny. It was as if his brain and body had been programmed for basketball.

The basketball season was starting. Teams were getting ready for the opening games. The Bankers, Dandyboy's team, was not the favorite to win the championship. Many thought it would be a long season for the Bankers.

Dandyboy was sitting in his room at home. He was gathering up his gear to go to practice. This was his last year. He was daydreaming. "Can we win this year," he murmured to himself. Just then Storymaster, his Guardfather, appeared.

"What's happening, Dandyboy?" Storymaster said in greeting Dandyboy.

"Not much, Storymaster," Dandyboy replied, "I'm getting ready for practice, but I was thinking there's no way we can win this year."

"Come on Dandy, you always say that."

"No, I mean it this time. James is gone, Willie is gone."

"So, you're ready to hang up the socks, are you?"

"That's not funny Storymaster," Dandyboy stated.

"Look Dandy, Willie was a star according to you but did you get to the championship?"

"Just remember Dandy, some teams with stars don't win. The star may soar but the real stars make their teams fly," Storymaster said as he left.

That day at practice, Dandyboy thought a lot about what Storymaster had said. When he arrived at home after his workout Storymaster was sitting on his bed.

"Storymaster, what did you mean when you said the real star makes his team fly?"

"Well, Dandy, it seems that the fans always remember who scored the most points or who made the greatest dunk, but Dandy, no championships are won by one guy scoring a lot of points or by the most thunderous dunks."

"Yeah, but it's nice to score a lot of points."

"Sure it is Dandy, and you've done that, but what about getting to the championship game, isn't that what it is all about?"

"I sure would like to win the championship, or even get to play in the championship game."

"You can Dandyboy, but it takes sacrifice, hard work, you've got to get the whole team involved."

"Dandyboy did you ever hear about the theory of the 'mesh'?" Storymaster inquired.

"Mesh? No, what's that?"

"Well, Dandyboy, sit right down and let the Storymaster tell you about the secret of the mesh," replied a smiling Storymaster.

"Many years ago in the NBA there were two great teams. One was the Left Coast Lakers. Charles Buyzall, their general manager, wanted desperately to win the championship. He wanted to dominate the league. Money was no object. He decided to buy the best players around. The first player he acquired was The Big Flipper. The Flipper was 7 feet tall and as strong as Hercules. Once he scored one hundred points in a game. The Flipper was intimidating.

"Buyzall thought, all I need now is a forward who can do it all. And there was such a player around. His name was E. Duzitall and he was the missing piece to the championship. So Buyzall did what he does the best, he bought Duzitall.

"'Now I have the championship,' Buyzall told the owners. 'Bring on the other team.'

"Although the Left Coast Lakers looked awesome on paper, for after all they had the three greatest scorers in the league on the team, would that produce a championship? Most fans said yes.

"However, on the other side of the continent there was one shrewd dude. He was Redbach, general manager and coach of the Bosstown Celts. For years his teams dominated the league and won many a championship. No one could figure out why. The fans knew that the Celts almost always won the championship, but few could tell you who their players were. There was never a scoring champ on the Bosstown team. Redbach had a secret. He knew the theory of the mesh."

Dandyboy was becoming impatient. All the stories about basketball that he had heard or read about dealt with high scorers or those who win a slam dunk contest. "Come on, Storymaster, what do you mean 'mesh,' is that some kind of secret play," Dandyboy inquired?

"Patience Dandyboy," replied Storymaster. "You cannot learn the secret of the mesh unless you are patient."

"Let me first tell you a little bit about Redbach. He was small by basketball standards. He wasn't quick. He couldn't shoot that well but whenever he played he seemed to win. Redbach could see the court. He knew where every player was. Redbach learned that matchups were more important than manpower. He learned that teamwork was more important than individual strength.

"You won't believe this, Dandyboy, but once he told me a story about something he learned as a small boy. He had

dropped an ice cream cone on the sidewalk. While he was standing there and looking at the ice cream cone and thinking about
what he should do, a crow flew down and tried to pick it up. It
was too heavy and the crow in frustration squawked and flew
away. As the bird departed, a small mouse raced over in anticipation of savoring a great delight. The small mouse, however, could
not move the cone to safe quarters free from other predators pil-
fering his prize, so he too scooted away. The next intruders were
a colony of ants. Their coordinated effort succeeded in removing
the ice cream cone from the sidewalk to the safety of their lair.

"Redbach told me he never forgot that episode. He believed
that teamwork was the key to success. Redbach never looks for
stars who are not willing to help in the quest for victory. His
plan called for the players to mesh into one efficient unit. Five
players playing as one unit could beat five players playing as
five separate units.

"In the next few years, the Left Coast Lakers managed to
win one championship, but all the others were won by Redbach
and his Celts."

"Storymaster," Dandyboy inquired, "can anyone learn the
mesh if they try?"

"Sure, Dandyboy, but most people don't try. They still
believe the way that Buyzall thinks, just get the individual star."

"Did anyone else ever learn about the mesh?"

"Yeah, one other team did," said Storymaster, "there was
this great city in the east. They had not won a championship.
The people were very forlorn. They prayed to all the gods for the
championship but it was always the Left Coast Lakers or the
Bosstown Celts who won.

"'Why can't the City Knicks win?' was the lament.

"Then a miracle occurred. The City Knicks hired a new
coach. His name was Crimsonman. He too had been a basketball

player. His stature and ability was like Redbach. He revered Redbach. Often he studied the game films of the Celts to see if he could learn the secret to their success.

"For a while Crimsonman proceeded as did the other teams of the league. His owner tried as Buyzall did to buy all the best players. It was senseless as the City Knicks were always beat out of the championships.

"One day Crimsonman had a dream. He saw a championship banner hoisted up to the rafters of Madtown Garden the home of the City Knicks. Crimsonman beard a voice, 'It is the mesh. It is the mesh that brings the banner to the Garden.' Crimsonman had learned the secret.

"The next day Crimsonman could hardly contain himself. He raced to the office of the owner. 'Boss,' he said, 'I've got the secret. We need the mesh.'

"The owner perplexed, said, 'What are you talking about? You look awful. You don't need the mesh, you need a night's sleep.

"'No boss, believe me, I had a dream I saw the championship banner in the rafters.'

"'Believe me, Crimsonman, you can't believe how many dreams I've had of that as well.'

"'But boss, I know how we can do it. We need the mesh. We need five players playing as one. I studied Redbach and that's what his teams always do.'

"'Okay, so get the mesh,' the owner responded, 'but how do you do that?'

"'We've got to get Dave Defense from the Motortown Pistons.'

"'How are we going to do that?'

"'We give them Bells and Howie.'

"'You must be delirious with fever. Give up our two best players?'

"'Yes boss, that's what we've got to do.'

"'Any other crazy ideas?'

"'Yup, I need the Jewel.'

"Well, Dandyboy, as it happened the boss of the City Knicks went out and traded Bells and Howie for Dave Defense and he bought the Jewel. Now the City Knicks were a unit. There was Princebill, a scholar and an athlete always moving, always playing defense. Ruler Read was a presence in the middle, he could check out anybody and he was the leader of the team. Slyfraz was at the center of the action. He could steal the ball, he could play defense, and he always saw the open man.

"The key, however, Dandyboy, was that they played like a unit. No individual stars, everybody helped out, and they played team defense. In fact, it so impressed the fans that the shout of 'De-fense' 'De-fense' originated at Madtown Garden. Defense is what led to the first championship for the City Knicks."

Dandyboy thought long and hard about what Storymaster said. It was true, the City Knicks finally won a championship. But could his team learn the mesh? Could they make it to the championship?

The season started and as Dandyboy had predicted, his team was truly without good players. In the beginning, however, Dandyboy could carry his team. Soon the day would come, however, where he needed the help of his teammates. So, Dandyboy tried hard to make each of the other players better. He passed the ball to them. He encouraged those who would rebound and dive for the loose balls. He even cheered them on when he was taken out of the game. Dandyboy became a team player for he wanted to create the mesh Storymaster had told him about.

He worked with Double S who would one day become a

star. Double S learned to shoot and dribble so he could help out when the other team double teamed Dandyboy. Slim Aaron learned to rebound and box out his man. He learned to look up court and throw the fast break pass. Everybody learned a role. Jeffmo worked on defense and how to set a pick. The team was starting to mesh.

The hard work paid off because the team was going to the playoffs. The true test would now begin. The first game would be against Russelman's team. They were big and powerful, much stronger than Dandyboy's team. They had muscled their way into the playoffs often intimidating the smaller opponents. It would be a challenge for Dandyboy and the Bankers.

Coach Davemetz called the team together. "Boys, I'm proud of you, you are beginning to play as a team. The game tonight will be real tough. Don't get into a pushing match with them. Pass the ball and cut."

"Coach, may I say a few words?" asked Dandyboy.

"Sure Dandy, go ahead."

"Guys, you've got to remember that they're going to double team me. Look for the pass from me and please make your shots," Dandyboy implored.

"What if they block my shot," chimed in Double S who was one of the starting players.

"Double S," said the coach, "everybody gets a shot blocked once in a while, don't let that stop you."

"These guys are so big," lamented Slim Aaron, "they're going to push me all over."

Dandyboy started to get angry, "Hey guys, that's not the way we play. We don't let anybody scare us. We play together and box out and help on defense. That's what we're going to do tonight. Just remember, they can't shoot as well as we can and we can run a lot faster."

The game was just as everyone anticipated. Russelman's

team, The Intimidators, began their taunting right from the beginning. Biggerboy, the Intimidators center blocked Double S's first shot and started his trash talk. The next time down the court, the Intimidators double teamed Dandyboy and when he looked for Double S to pass the ball to, Double S was looking away. It appeared like he didn't want the ball. Dandyboy was forced to throw up an errant shot.

Slim Aaron, who was under the boards and who should have rebounded, saw Biggerboy and Russelman coming toward the basket and he bailed out. Russelman got the rebound, went the length of the court, and scored a basket. Dandyboy was furious. Why had his teammates given up? What was all this stuff about the mesh and unity? He decided to take things into his own hands.

The first half was a furious battle between the heroics of Dandyboy and the strength of the Intimidator. The Intimidators were leading by two points at halftime. It was obvious that Dandyboy could not do it on his own and unless someone aroused the rest of the team, the Bankers would never get to the championship game.

Coach Davemetz tried his best to get the team to focus but it looked like Double S and Slim Aaron were too frightened to make any contribution. On the Intimidators side of the court the urgings of their coach could be heard.

"Boys," said Coach Hollersloud, "all of the Bankers but Dandyboy have quit. If we can knock him out of the game, we win in a walk."

Russelman and Biggerboy looked at each other. They knew what they had to do. On the first play of the second half, as Dandyboy drove for the basket, he was sandwiched by Biggerboy and Russelman. Dandyboy went down with a thud. The gym grew silent. Was Dandyboy hurt? Would he have to leave the game? Coach Davemetz ran out onto the court.

Dandyboy nodded his head. "I'm going to send someone in for you," the coach continued.

"No way," said Dandyboy, "nobody is going to shoot my foul shots, not after I get hit like that."

In the turmoil following Dandyboy's two foul shots he looked at his teammates.

"Guys, look they can't hurt us. I took their hardest shot and I'm okay. You can't let them intimidate you. I'm begging you, please help me, I need you guys."

The players, Double S, Slim Aaron, Jeffmo, and Justin, all looked at Dandyboy. How could they let him down? Up to now he had single-handedly kept them in the game.

"Dandy, nobody's gonna push me around," snarled Slim Aaron.

"Yeah, me neither," said Jeffmo.

Even Double S, who is usually so reserved, got a look of determination in his eye.

When the Bankers took the floor after the time out, they were a determined group.

Jeffmo, who was guarding Russelman, stole the ball from him and passed it to Dandyboy. As Dandyboy moved toward the basket, the Intimidators double-teamed him. Out of the corner of his eye he saw Double S cut down the lane. A bounce pass ended up in Double S's hands. He turned toward the basket as Biggerboy closed in on him. Double S pump faked and Biggerboy went flying past him. Double S laid the ball up for an easy two points.

On the next play after Russelman missed a jump shot, Slim Aaron, who had positioned himself under the basket, boxed out the massive Biggerboy and gobbled the rebound. A quick outlet pass to Dandyboy was the start of the fast break that was finished off with a reverse layup by Dandyboy.

From that point on, the game for all practical purposes was

over. The Bankers had gained confidence and in the process had totally undermined the game plan of the Intimidators. Coach Hollersloud could not inspire his team to turn the game around. Final score: Bankers 52, Intimidators 40.

A bruised but happy Dandyboy returned home to rest and prepare for tomorrow's game. As he placed his weary body on his bed he was about to drop off to sleep when there was a knock on his bedroom door.

"Dandyboy," said Storymaster, "how's the superstar? That was some game tonight."

"Some superstar I am," responded Dandyboy. "I almost got knocked out of the game and if Jeffmo didn't steal the ball, or if Double S didn't score or Slim Aaron didn't rebound, we'd have lost. I'm not a superstar."

"Well, Dandy, you have to know what I mean by superstar. Let me tell you a story that might illustrate what I mean."

"Once there was a team called the Chitown Tauruses. They had the greatest basketball play who ever lived. He could do everything. His name was Air M. He could soar and glide and no one could hang with him. Air M scored more points than anyone in the league yet the Tauruses never won the championship.

"He often wondered why. He longed for the day when he could wear the ring of a champion, but as hard as he tried, it did not happen.

"Then, one day a spiritual leader came to the team. He was called Soaring Eagle. He had played for the City Knicks when Crimsonman was the coach. He learned much from Crimsonman including the mesh. Soaring Eagle knew that he must teach Air M another truth, however.

"So, in his first meeting with Air M, Soaring Eagle said, 'Air M, to win the prize you must be a superstar.'

"Air M answered, 'But I am a star, everyone calls me a star.'

"'No,' said Soaring Eagle. 'It is true you are a star, but you are not a superstar. For to be a superstar, one must elevate the play of those around him to a level they could not reach without his help. To be a superstar, you must make stars of those around you.'

"Now Air M was a thoughtful man. He took the lesson from Soaring Eagle with him. He thought about it for a long time. When Air M finally understood the truth of the words of Soaring Eagle the ring became his. In time he and his teammates won three such rings."

"So, Dandyboy when I called you a superstar I meant it as in the way Soaring Eagle spoke to Air M. Today you made those around you into stars and that is why you are a superstar."

Dandyboy's eyes were closed as the last words were spoken by Storymaster. The sleep would be good for tomorrow would bring about another challenge.

The final game of the Division One playoff would be against the Pitbulls. They were the last team to make the playoffs. The Pitbulls had upset two higher seeded teams to get to this position. Many teams that had taken them lightly had suffered the indignity of loss because of that attitude.

The Pitbulls featured a very large lumbering boy known to all as Tank. He had no finesse but once he got the ball and started toward the basket, few would challenge his approach to the hoop for fear of being trampled. The other key to their success was the back court tandem of the twin terrors, literally twins known not too affectionately around the league as Dumb and Dumber. They were a tenacious pair who constantly harried and harassed opponents. Though small of stature, they were fearless and gladly sacrificed their bodies for the sake of victory. Often they would not be around for the end of the game because of the rule that required a player to sit down after a fifth foul.

Miraculously they had avoided this distinction during the playoffs. Some speculated that the officials would allow a more open style of play in the playoffs, and the protection normally given to players would be reduced to allow the game to be played in that manner. Coach Davemetz worried about this because the Roller Derby style of play of the Pitbulls usually kept the score close and the Pitbulls were always capable of scoring an upset if they could stay close to their opponent going into the final quarter.

During the first half of the game the Bankers looked invincible. They passed the ball well. They prevented Tank from getting the ball and they managed to avoid the grabbing, holding, pushing style of the twins. At halftime the Bankers were ahead by ten points and it could have been more if a couple of their shots had not rolled out of the basket.

"One more half of good basketball," Coach Davemetz said, "and we end up in the championship game. Remember, Dandy has to sit out this quarter so you guys have to be careful. Let's not let them get on a roll."

The team huddled and clasped hands. On the designated number they shouted "Defense." Well, nothing could be further from the truth. The team seemed to be sleep walking and before you knew it, the Pitbulls were nipping at the heels of the Bankers. They managed to close the score to two points when the fourth quarter was to begin. The worst fears of Coach Davemetz were realized. The Pitbulls had been allowed to remain close going into the fourth quarter.

On the other sideline, the Pitbulls were joyful. Coach "Bull Dog" Bradley was barking orders to the team. "Twins, you've got to shut Dandyboy down this quarter. You've got to be on him like white on rice. I don't ever want you away from him."

The energetic twins were almost beyond control. This is

what they did the best. The question was what would the officials do. It became apparent after the first play that they would do very little to control the tempo of the game.

On a designated play from the sideline, Dandyboy received the inbound pass from Slim Aaron, moved around a pick set by Jeffmo, and dribbled to the basket. His layup kissed off the glass and spun in for two points. Dumb and Dumber were holding him but the officials refused to blow the whistle.

Coach Davemetz rose to his feet and shouted something to the official but to no avail. On the next play Tank got the ball and scored for the Pitbulls. No one would step in front of him and he went unimpeded to the hoop.

Baskets continued to be exchanged and with one minute left the Pitbulls tied the score. Coach Davemetz signaled for a time out.

"What's going on out there?" shouted the coach.

"They're holding me and the official is doing nothing," said Dandyboy.

"Well, what do you want me to do, go out on the court and stop them, Dandyboy?" the coach responded sarcastically.

Dandyboy looked at him disdainfully, then in a quiet confident manner said to the coach, "Let me have the ball, I'll get it done coach, even if all five of them hold me."

The team, inspired by Dandyboy's words, raced out on the court. The inbound pass came to Dandyboy and he methodically worked the ball up the right side of the court. When he reached halfcourt, he reversed the ball to his left hand, broke the double team and beat Tank to the hoop for a goal. It was an awesome display of basketball skill.

Dandyboy did not hustle back to midcourt for defense. Instead he turned quickly around and stole the inbound pass and drove in for a layup. As he went up for the shot, he was crashed into by Dumb and Dumber. Miraculously the ball went through the hoop and to the pleasure of Coach Davemetz the sound of the whistle pierced the air. The official signaled a good hoop and a foul shot.

Dandyboy swished the foul shot. The Bankers now led by five with thirty seconds left. In their haste to score, Tank dribbled the ball off his foot. Slim Aaron picked up the ball and passed it off to Dandyboy. Dandyboy, intent upon running out the clock, dribbled the ball toward the center of the court when he was grabbed by Dumb or Dumber, no one could tell the difference between them. The officials signal that a foul had been committed. Dandyboy sank both shots and the game ended.

Coach "Bulldog" Bradley, in consoling his troops, told them they played great, "You guys should be proud of the fact that you held Dandyboy to sixteen points." That was quite a compliment but Dandyboy was too excited by the victory and the prospect 6f a championship game to take much pleasure from the remark.

That night Storymaster appeared at bedtime to tell one more fable to Dandyboy.

"Will we win tomorrow, Guardfather? Will I get the championship?" queried Dandyboy.

"I don't know Dandy, but let me ask you a question. If you knew you were going to lose would you still play the game?"

Dandyboy looked perplexed, he started to speak but was interrupted by the Storymaster. "Before you answer Dandy, let me tell you a story."

"In a time when the world seemed upside down, when war raged and innocent people were killed and imprisoned, two brave courageous men stood up to the forces of evil. Each behaved and performed in different ways. One, whose name was Victory spoke out against the evil influence. He tried to arouse others to stand up as well. Victory was imprisoned for his statements and was not heard from. Many thought he had been killed by the savage evil people. Victory had been married to a beautiful young woman. She idolized her brave husband. Her name was Ingrid.

"The other man, Ric, was something of a mystery. He worked in a quieter manner. He was not outspoken, his deeds spoke for him. He tried to bring little attention to himself. Nevertheless, his activities against the forces of evil became known. Ric became a wanted fugitive. He became a hunted man.

"When reports of the death of Victory, the spokesman for good, were given to his wife she was devastated. Ingrid decided to take up the cause for peace her husband had pursued. In her desire to carry on this work, Ingrid met the other freedom fighter. They tell in love. Shortly thereafter, the evil people discovered Ric's whereabouts. Ric learned they were in hot pursuit of him. He and Ingrid planned to escape to Morocco. They were to meet at the train station. Ingrid failed to show up. Ric, heartbroken, was forced to flee alone.

"While in Morocco, Ric continued his good work under a disguise. He opened a nightclub. Ric always wondered why Ingrid did not show up. As it turned out Victory, who was presumed dead, had in fact escaped from prison. On the day she was to have left with Ric, Victory's friends sent word to his wife that he was alive. She, although now in love with Ric, knew that her duty was to Victory. She had to get him to freedom and to a place where he could lead the good people against the evil empire. The only way to accomplish this was to get to Morocco and then to safety. She was committed to get Victory to a place where he could lead the world to victory.

"In Morocco she again met Ric at his nightclub. When Ric saw her he was very upset. Of all the places in the world why did she pick mine, Ric said to himself. How could she have left him and not met him at the train station? Ric was very selfish. He hated himself for ever having loved the woman.

"At night Ingrid came to see Ric, she begged him to help Victory. Ingrid pledged her undying love and commitment to Ric, if he would only provide for Victory's safe passage to the free world. Ric, although still in love with Ingrid, now realized that the woman was more important to Victory and his good work than to him. Risking his own life, Ric arranged for their safe passage to freedom even though he knew his love for the woman would be lost forever.

"So, Dandy, is it the same with you? Would it be better to play the game, even if you were to lose, than to never have played the game at all?"

"Oh, Guardfather, yes! Yes! I would gladly play the game over and over again even if we were to lose! Yes I do believe it would be better to play and lose than never to have played at all," Dandyboy responded.

"You are wise beyond your years, Dandyboy. Ric too knew it was better to have loved and lost than to never have loved at all."

And so it came to pass that Dandyboy played the championship game. It was a thrilling game. The Bankers were losing early in the game but came on with a rush at the end. Double S scored points. Slim Aaron rebounded against taller opponents. Jeffmo played in-your-face defense. Dandyboy scored and passed and rebounded and played D. It was a glorious game. It was thrilling game.

With ten seconds left in the game, the Bankers were behind by one point. It was their ball under their own basket. Jeffmo inbounded the ball to Dandyboy. He dribbled up court, the crowd was screaming, "He doesn't have time to get off a shot." "Even if he has time it is too far away," screamed another. Not a fan was seated. Dandy wove past the first defender, and cut back toward midcourt, a behind-the-back dribble took him around two defenders, eight seconds, seven seconds, six seconds, the clock wound down. With one second on the clock, Dandyboy stopped, he sprang into the air, and launched a shot toward the basket. The buzzer sounded, there was silence as the ball fell toward the basket and victory . . . or defeat . . . but it did not matter for it was just better to have played the game.